Adam and the Magic Marble

by

Adam and Carol Buehrens

Adam and the Magic Marble

by *Adam and Carol Buehrens*

Published by: ☐┬◯ **Hope Press** P.O.Box 188
Duarte, CA 91009-0188 U.S.A.
SAN 200-3244

Other books on Tourette syndrome by Hope Press:
Tourette Syndrome and Human Behavior
by *David E. Comings, M.D.*
**Ryan – A Mother's Story of Her Hyperactive/ Tourette
Syndrome Child** by *Susan Hughes*
Hi, I'm Adam by *Adam Buehrens*
(to order see back leaf)

Printed in the United States of America

Library of Congress Cataloging-in-Publication Data

Buehrens, Adam, 1980-
 Adam and the magic marble / by Adam and Carol Buehrens.
  p. cm.
 Summary: Two boys with Tourette syndrome find a magic marble that can cure their disorder but decide that their friend with cerebral palsy needs th marble more than they do.
  ISBN 1-878267-30-2 : $6.95
  [1. Tourette syndrome -- Fiction. 2. Friendship--Fiction.]
I. Buehrens, Carol, 1954 . II. Title.
P27.B885Ad 1991
[Fic] --dc20
90-2390
CIF
A

A Note About Tourette Syndrome

Two of the boys in this story have Tourette syndrome. This is a common hereditary disorder whose most prominent symptoms are muscle tics such as rapid eyeblinking, facial grimacing, shoulder shrugging, head jerking and others; and vocal noises such as throat clearing, snorting, sniffing, spitting, humming and others. In addition to tics individuals with Tourette syndrome may have difficulty with temper tantrums, learning disorders, hyperactivity, conduct, anxiety and other behavioral problems.

For more information about this intriguing disorder see *Tourette Syndrome and Human Behavior* by David E. Comings, M.D. and *RYAN - A Mother's Story of Her Hyperactive/Tourette Syndrome Child* by Susan Hughes. They can be ordered from Hope Press using the form in the back flyleaf.

Cerebral palsy is a birth defect characterized by spastic muscles and often results in difficulty walking or talking.

Acknowledgments

The authors would like to thank the following people:

Lora Buehrens, for being a character in the book and for helping her brother during difficulties. She always has a kind word of understanding for Adam, and as she says, "she will always be his sister their whole life."

Chris Parsons for being a character in our book, and for being a special friend to Adam.

Mrs. Melanie Sowa and her fifth grade class of 1990-1991, at Jasper Elementary School, Alta Loma, California. We appreciate the time they took in reading our book, sending us many letters filled with their comments, and being our special "editors."

Joanie and Rick Valasek of Quicktype & Design, Anaheim, California, for helping us with the production of the computer artwork for the cover.

Chapter 1.

Splishin' N' Splashin'

I didn't really want to go to the party. It would be a lot of grownups sitting by the pool, gabbing to each other. Real boring.

Mom had said that there would be a lot to eat, but I knew it would be stuff like salad, vegetables and the things grownups like to eat as they sit around a pool. If there was any cake or cookies, I probably couldn't eat it. Sometimes my mom thinks that sugar makes me shake more. Well, sort of twitch. The reason I twitch is because I have Tourette syndrome, not because I eat any sugar. Tourette is kind of like a handicap that makes you tic when you don't want to (like shake your head, blink your eyes, stick out your tongue or even spit), but I'll explain more later. In fact, all of the kids there had Tourette syndrome. I really worried about that. I mean, what would it be like seeing other kids with the same kind of problems I had? I thought I might be embarassed or that other kids would laugh at me. I don't know what I thought actually. I just know I was scared to be there.

When I got to the party it wasn't all that bad. Sure the adults were talking, but the kids there were pretty fun. None of them laughed at me, and everyone just ignored each other's tics. The adults were in a good mood and no one was yelling at us kids, even when we splashed them. I think they were trying to show each other that they were good parents and that they never got mad.

Anyway, I got to swim all afternoon. Swimming that day was real important because it must have been 100 degrees in the shade! The only place it was cool was in the water.

The party was also pretty good because I met a kid there named Chris. Our folks were hoping that we would like each other, partly because we would be going to school together and partly because Chris has Tourette syndrome also. Chris was a real funny guy and I liked him right away. At first I didn't know what to make of him. When he had a tic, his whole body shook. The only thing that didn't shake was one leg. I didn't say anything though, mainly because one of my tics at the time made my whole head roll back and he acted like he didn't notice.

Well, we had a blast throwing ourselves into the water and making dive-bombs. This cracked us up because the adults were sitting real close to the edge of the pool, but none of them had bathing suits on (they were kind of dressed up). They were getting pretty soaked. One of my splashes made a lady wet from head to foot and she never said a thing. Those parents were acting extra special today. I was just glad that she wasn't my mom, since I would probably get it when I got home for getting her all wet.

I should tell you a little about Tourette syndrome. Not too much, though. I don't want you to think that I'm weird or anything. My mom explained to me that it is a neurological disorder, whatever that is. Like I told you, it makes me twitch and do funny things like that. But, Tourette also can make you get stuck in a rut, and I repeat things over and over (boy, do I ever!). Sometimes I even go into a rage. And I mean RAGE. A rage is like you threw a tantrum that got out of hand. I don't have rages usually, but when I do, WATCH OUT! I can't stop myself at all. My mom has it figured out that she just gets out of my way. I have to go to my room until I calm down.

I take medicine for my Tourettes, which I wear as a patch on my skin (usually on my back). I just started wearing my medicine this summer. It really helps, so now I hardly have big problems like rages. I still tic though.

One time a little boy down the street asked me what the patch was. I had my shirt off and it must have looked like a pretty big bandage or something. Well, he's real little and I thought I would tell him about my medicine, but he kept saying it looked like I was hurt bad. He seemed to want a good story, so I told him that it was a shark bite.

That surprised him, and he wanted to hear more. I continued by telling him that I was being used for shark bait. You should of seen his face. He bought the whole thing. I mean, he was only about 5 years old. The problem was that his mom heard me telling my story, and she told my mom. I learned real fast about telling stories about my medicine and everything. So what I'm telling you now is the truth.

It was interesting to meet so many kids with Tourette. There were seven other kids at the party, all twitching away at each other and pretending not to notice. We were lucky because no one threw a tantrum or got in a fight with each other. I thought this would happen since I figured everyone with Tourette had real short tempers and the day was very hot. But the most exciting thing that happened was when Susie walked into the bathroom when Tim was in there, and she ran out and told everyone that she saw him. Of course, we didn't really care, but he was furious when he got out. He hid in the corner until his mom made him get back in the pool. That seemed to be the most exciting thing, except of course that I met Chris and we were going to be friends at school.

Chapter 2.

The Belching King

On the first morning that school started, my little sister Lora and I went down to the bus stop early. If I had known what was going to happen, we wouldn't have gotten there before the bus. I was dressed in my new school clothes and had even combed my hair. As we walked up, I realized that a boy named Joe was already there. Joe isn't a nice kid. In fact, he's the kind of kid that would tie a string to the tail of a cat and then laugh when the poor thing ran around in circles trying to catch it. The problem was, he wouldn't stop there. Next he would tie a stick to the cat's tail, and then a rock, anything he could find. He just doesn't know when to stop. And that's just what he does to cats. He's really cruel when it comes to 10 year old boys who have their hair combed just right and have a tic.

Well, Lora was only seven years old and was real worried about being at the bus stop with Joe. So she and I walked up real slowly so that we could buy some extra time. I figured the other kids would get there soon, so if we stalled maybe they would show up. Maybe Joe wouldn't pick on me in front of the other kids.

When we got to the corner, it was strange because he didn't say a thing to us. He just looked at Lora and me real hard, squinting with his eyebrows drawn low, and then went on with what he was doing, which was smashing ants with his foot. We were beginning to think we were safe, until I saw Joe's friends, Tom and Sid, walk up behind him.

"What ya doin' Joe?" asked Tom, looking at me the whole while. "Is Adam you're friend now? You hangin' with the wimp that tics?"

"No way," Joe stood up straight and you could see that he must have put on 3 inches this summer, and gained about 20 pounds. "I was just thinkin' about squishing him like these ants, and rubbing him into the dirt real hard." Then he let out a loud, long "BELCH!" This was not a little burp. This was a full-on belch. Joe always belched, he didn't care who was around and who heard him. He was the "belching king."

Now Tom and Joe were in the 6th grade, just one year over me. But they both were at least a head taller. Sid was only a 3rd grader, which meant he was still pretty little, but he was the dirtiest little kid you ever saw. Even on the first day of school he looked like he had worn the same clothes for a week already, and slept in them every night too. I didn't want to tangle with these kids. I spent the whole last year avoiding them, hiding behind doors and ducking into classrooms whenever they came by.

One time last year they got me on the playground and started pushing me. They grabbed me and pushed my face into the dirt. There was dirt in my mouth and I started spitting it out. That's when I blew up. I got my Tourette temper so bad that I began yelling and screaming out so many cuss words, ones I didn't even know that I knew. I started repeating them over and over until my face turned red.

That's the problem when you have Tourettes. You start in on something then you can't stop. You just keep repeating and repeating. A teacher came out and grabbed me, but I kept yelling those words. It was awful. I was screaming those cuss words as she pulled me down the hall to the main office.

We went right past a girl that I like named Teresa, and her mouth dropped open hearing all those words coming from me. I must have looked like quite a sight, dirt all over my face, spitting mud out, crying and yelling words I can't repeat now. I couldn't stop till I threw cold water on my face. Then I fell asleep in the nurses office. Well, Tom and Joe and Sid were all in trouble, and I got to sleep it off. As you can imagine, they have been trying to get back at me ever since. In fact, I think I was about to find out what they had been saving for me all summer.

Tom starts it. "So the baby wants to cry," he shouts, and up comes his fist full of dirt, in my general direction. "Let's see if you can eat dirt for us now!"

"The baby gets dirty!" said Sid. It was apparent that he took extreme pleasure tossing his hand full of dirt, throwing it more in the air than on me.

"This will get you now!" said Joe, adding his 2 cents worth. But, Joe grabs the dirt at his feet which was full of ants. By now, I've been able to get some distance between me and these guys, and Joe throws his fist of dirt and ants at me. Luckily, his ants missed me completely, but all of a sudden Joe screams out in agony. "Damned ants! Ants all over me!" And indeed, you could see them crawling all over him. The big red kind. The kind that like to sting. He was hopping all around, hitting himself crazy-like.

I had dirt in my hair and on my new clothes, so I should have been upset. But I couldn't help it, I had to laugh. It was the funniest thing I had ever seen. Joe was hopping all around, screaming. Tom and Sid were hitting him all over, trying to beat the ants off. It was great. I was laughing so hard I didn't notice that the rest of the kids had arrived and were now standing there waiting for the bus, laughing at Joe. Joe was getting pretty angry, and he was probably figuring it was all my fault.

"You gotta tell Dad," Lora was whispering in my ear. "You gotta tell him so that we don't have to come to the bus stop again."

Well, this was all pretty exciting. Yet, I

knew I had to think about what Lora said. I suddenly had to shake all over and I think I rolled my head back nine or ten times from my Tourettes before we got on the bus. I made sure we sat clear up front so that no funny business could happen out of the driver's ear-shot. This was a good move because Joe, Tom, and Sid went clear to the back. I looked back and there was Joe, all twitching with pain, red lumps on his arms already swelling from bites. I thought, "Good, let him twitch for awhile and see how he likes it," but I figured this wasn't a good thought. My twitching and tics aren't painful. And then I thought, "Oh well, it serves him right."

Chapter 3.

The Perfect Teacher

I guess I thought this year would be different. I thought that somehow people would look at me and I would be able to hear them say "Isn't Adam cute this year? Boy, Adam is great, isn't he?" Instead, I walked down the hall and no one noticed me. That bugged me, because I had really changed. I was older and a little taller. I had been on the swim team this summer and won a lot of ribbons. Surely someone could tell I was different just by looking at me. Couldn't they see how hard I've worked at controlling my tics? Now that I'm on medication, couldn't they see how I'm acting better?

But, of course they couldn't. That's the real strange thing about summer vacations. When they're over, it's just like they never happened. School starts and everything's the same, just like you never left for summer vacation at all.

Chris was waiting for me by our classroom. He is actually a real cool looking kid. He's tall, at least 3 inches taller than me. And he hasd blond hair that was sort of long and wavy. He even dressed cool. He was wearing those neat sneakers that you can push the little tongue on them and it blows air into the shoe to make them fit just right. These are the greatest shoes in all the world.

"Hi Adam," Chris said, and then he grimmaced as his body shook all over,   except, of course, for his one leg. "Darn, I thought this tic would go away before school started."

That's the funny thing about Tourettes, you never know when a tic is going to come or go, when it is going to change or what your next tic will be. I've been rolling my head for a while now, but I've just started a tic that wiggles my fingers. In fact, I'm kind of worried about holding a pencil and ticking my fingers at the same time.

Just then I saw trouble around the corner. "Be careful, Chris. Don't tic now," I whispered as low as I could so that Tom and Joe couldn't hear me as they walked towards us. "These guys would have a field day if they see us tic." You could hear Joe let out a belch as they got closer.

Chris held real still and didn't shake at all, and we quickly slipped into our classroom. Tom and Joe walked right by, but not without spitting at me first. I was glad he missed my foot, and all of a sudden I remembered about the dirt they threw at me earlier.

"Chris, quick. Check me out. Do I have dirt all over me?" Chris did a quick one-two check, brushed my shoulders, and passed me off as okay.

We looked for our seats. In fifth grade the teachers still figure out your seat assignments for you, and every desk had a name on it. Our names were somewhere in this classroom. Finally I found mine, with ADAM B. written in big bold letters on a paper that was placed on top of a mountain of books. It was in front of the whole classroom. Chris found his over to the right, by the big screen TV. I definitely liked Chris' seat better. It would be pretty great to sit in front of the TV. In fact, that was the best seat in the house.

"Good morning, children." All teachers have to say that in the morning of the first day of school. It is a law. "My name is Mrs. Keller, and I'm your teacher this year." Of course, we had all figured this out by now, but I guess they have to say that too. Mrs. Keller sat very straight in her chair. "I just want to start out this year perfectly, because, as you may have heard, I'm perfect. I'm perfect in every way, shape, and form, so I never, never make a mistake." There was a glint in her eyes as she said that, a slight smile at the corners of her mouth. I was waiting for something, something to happen. How could she say she was perfect? "So, I'm glad to have you in my 6th grade class here at Glentable".

MRS. KELLER

Sixth grade, did she say 6th grade? Did she say Glentable? This is Brookstone! I looked at Chris, and I could see his face was all bunched up. He was going to laugh, but the whole class was silent. He couldn't hold it in any longer. "Hah, hah! This isn't the 6th grade!" All eyes were on him. I started laughing too, and then the whole class was roaring. I couldn't tell if they were laughing at the teacher or at Chris, but as soon as the teacher joined in I knew that we were all laughing together.

"Well, don't tell anybody I made this mistake. It will only be our secret that I'm not perfect, okay? I mean, what would everyone do if they didn't think I was perfect? I guess that none of us are, really. So don't be worried if you make a few mistakes in my classroom. That's what we're here for this year, to learn, isn't it." Mrs. Keller smiled at us and I knew instantly I would like her.

After lunch, Chris and I discovered we were out on the playground the same time as the 6th graders. That meant "Bully alert." We had to keep our eyes out for Joe and Tom. Sid was just in the 3rd grade and didn't have lunch period the same time as us.

I saw them before Chris did, but obviously not before they had seen us. Tom and Joe were already on there way over, walking like bullies, looking like bullies. Yes, I could see that Joe had his eyebrows drawn real low over his eyes, looking kind of like a bull-dog. "Oh shoot, they're coming over."

Chris had never met these guys before. I don't think he fully appreciated the situation.

"Oh, those kids don't look so tough," he said as he walked slightly toward them. "I bet they pick their nose and eat their boogers."

This was not the time to laugh, but I couldn't help it. Of course, now they were just about 10 feet from us, so it looked as though I was laughing in their faces. I knew this wouldn't be a pretty sight.

Tom came right over to me and grabbed me by my collar. The words, "What are you laughing at?" rumbled from his mouth as he pulled me up at least two inches from the ground.

Chapter 4.

The Magic Marble

Well, there we were out on the playground, me halfway into the air, Tom holding me up by my collar. I thought I was a goner.

"You little scum," Tom snarled at me, "I'm gonna get you now!"

And with that, I was thrown into the air

and I came down on the ground with a loud "thump." My hands hit so hard into the dirt that the fingers on my right hand stung as though they were sitting on a hot coal. "You jerk!" I yelled, "You jerk, you jerk, you jerk." Of course, now I couldn't stop because of my Tourettes. "You jerk, you jerk, see what you did!"

I clenched my fist in the dirt, gathering handfuls of soil. My right hand burned as I felt something hard in it. I thought it must be a rock, a nice size rock that could do some damage when I threw it. I pulled up my right hand and slung whatever was in my hand at him. Out flew the dirt, sand, and the hard thing.

That was when I saw "it" for the first time. It glowed a blinding light and made a whistling sound as it sailed towards Tom. It flew straight as though it was shot from a gun. I couldn't quite tell what it was, it being so bright and everything happening so fast. But I'll never forget the light. Whatever "it" was hit Tom hard on his forehead, and sent him down to the ground with a low moan.

That was all we heard from Tom for the rest of lunch recess. Just a low, painful moan as he laid there, real pitiful like, with dirt and grass all around him. That was about all Joe could take, and off he ran down the play yard toward the buildings. He left Tom just lying there. We could hear a faint "belch" as Joe disappeared among the buildings.

"What should we do now?" Chris asked, staring at me in amazement. "I think you killed him. What on earth did you throw at him anyway?"

I could see Chris searching the ground for the murder weapon. If it was there, it was no longer glowing. "I don't know. I had it in my hand. I just fell on it I guess." I could hardly speak. I felt as if I were frozen in time, my ears ringing, as though I were going to just drop dead away. And then I saw it again. It was sitting only a few feet from me. It must have bounced off of Tom's big old forehead and landed back by me. Now I could take time to examine it. I scrambled towards it on my knees.

"Chris look! I found it. It looks like, like, a little crystal ball or something." I noticed, as I picked it up, that it was clear as glass and hot feeling, I guess from the glow. It caught the light of the sun and sparkled as I held it up.

"Looks more like a marble to me," said a strange voice. I looked up to see a kid sitting in a wheelchair. "You knocked out that big guy with a plain old marble!" he added.

"Knocked him out? Yea, I guess I did." Tom moaned again. "I think he's comin' out of it. We better get out of here."

The three of us, Chris, me, and the kid in the wheelchair, headed toward the school buildings. Just as we hit the blacktop, the bell rang signaling the end of lunch recess. I turned around to look at Tom and there he was, sitting up and trying to get on his feet. When we got to the buildings, I turned around to look back again. Tom was walking now, dazed-like, tripping over his feet a little. But he was probably okay, since he always tripped over his feet a little. I knew I was really in for it now.

"My name's Matt," said the kid in the wheelchair. "I'm in your class." He whizzed past me and you could see that he really got around on that thing. "Maybe you didn't see me. I sit in the back."

He was right that I didn't see him, in fact, I hadn't noticed him all morning. But then again, I sit in the very front and I don't want to turn around much, since everyone would be able to see my eyes twitching from my Tourettes.

Chris introduced us to him. "My name is Chris and this is Adam," he said. "Hey, Adam, did you see that Tom guy's eyes roll back when you clobbered him with the marble. I thought I was going to wet my pants! Do ya still have the marble? Let me see it."

"Sure, but I don't think it's just a plain old marble. I think it must be magic or something. It was glowing like it was on fire." I handed the marble over to Chris, who took it and held it up to the sun. He squinted like he was looking through it.

"Maybe you just thought it was glowing. Maybe it just caught the sunlight," Matt said. He was trying to come up with a logical excuse for the strange light. "Maybe it just looked that way because you were scared and you hit the ground so hard."

"Maybe nothin'," my voiced squeaked as I protested. "I wasn't scared and I know what I saw."

"Can I hold it till after school?" Chris asked, playing with the marble in his hand.

"Sure, but don't lose it," I answered, still thinking about Tom laying on the playground. Then I remembered how hot the dirt felt just before I threw the marble at him. I thought my right hand was scraped in the dirt from my fall. But now, looking at it, my hand was fine. Could it be that the marble was hot, glowing with heat, as I threw it?

Chapter 5.

Chris' Magic Shakes

That afternoon, sitting in my classroom, I felt so strange. I wasn't sure if it was my Tourette syndrome or just the events of lunchtime. I had to excuse myself and go sit in the backroom, away from everyone and where it was quiet. It is very important that there is a quiet place for me to go to when I feel like I am having a problem with my Tourette. It is nice that our classroom has a back room (it is really a large storage closet with a desk that my teacher fixed up for me).

Last year, I had to walk all the way to the nurse's office when I didn't feel right. It was real hard walking all that way when I was having problems. I also didn't like it because people would be looking at me and ask me what I was doing.

But this year it's a lot better. I can walk real fast to the back room without having to say anything. In the back room, I can let all of my tics go without anyone seeing. I can put my head down on the desk and rest. I can also do my reading or math without anyone else staring at me or making noises. This really helps, because any distraction, and, "BAM," I might be in a rage or crying or something. And, like now, I can think extra hard on something. What I was thinking about was that marble.

How could I have knocked out Tom with a little marble? How could the marble glow? How did it make the dirt hot? What is so special about this marble? Is it really magic?

After school Chris, Matt, and I met by the front office. "Let's look at that marble again," Matt insisted we walk around the corner so no one could see. "Still looks like a plain marble to me. It doesn't look magic at all."

"Well, maybe not, but something's weird about it. Give it here." I grabbed the marble out of Matt's hand. "Looks special to me," I said as I held it up to the light, nodding my head as though I saw something that Chris must have missed when he looked at it. "Looks real special."

"What looks so special?" a voice grumbled from behind me.

I could recognize that voice anywhere – Tom. As I turned around I hid the marble behind me. There was Tom, with Joe and Sid right behind him. They looked like a gruesome threesome. I felt a hard lump in my throat. I couldn't swallow. My hand felt hot where I held the marble. I quickly backhanded it to Chris. "Nothin. Nothin looks special."

Matt rolled his wheelchair right up in front, pushing between Tom and me. "Leave us alone," he said "You better leave us alone or Adam will knock you out again." For some unforeseen reason, Matt was taunting him. "Watch out," he went on, "or Adam will let you have it."

"We're not afraid of Adam, the wimp," Joe snarled. "In fact, we're going to mince you all into dog meat!"

I guess Sid wanted to get into the fight. "Yeah," he said, and pushed Matt real hard. Matt's wheelchair fell over and Matt spilled out onto the cement.

That was when Chris went into action. I never saw anything like it. He shook. He stamped. All of his tics rolled into one and his body lunged forward. He was such a sight, we all were silent. Sid quickly darted between

Tom and Joe. Their eyes were opened so wide
you could see the whites all around them.

Then it happened. Chris's finger pointed
out toward the boys and it glowed with a
bright, fiery light. A noise came out of his
finger that sounded like a loud "CRACK," and
what looked like a   lightening bolt struck out
straight to Sid, Tom, and Joe. They   glowed
together like a Christmas tree.

The most magical thing I have ever seen
was happening.

The boys crackled.

The boys smoked.

The boys were shrinking!

They were changing shape!

They were...turning green?

THEY WERE TURNING INTO
FROGS!

Their skins became tight and glossy. Their mouths widened. Their eyes bumped out of the top of their heads. Suddenly the three boys were gone, and all that remained were three, green, slimey frogs.

"Chris, what did you do?" I asked, but I could see his eyes were wide with amazement. He didn't know either. "What are we going to do now?"

Matt was still on the ground, but he had already thought of our next move. "Catch them, catch them quick before they get away."

Chris and I scrambled to grab the frogs before they could hop out of our reach.

"Got'em! What are we going to do with them?" All of us looked at each other. What were we going to do?

Chapter 6.

Frogs, Frogs, Frogs

We didn't know what we were going to do with those three frogs. They were trying to hop away and were real hard to hold onto. I squeezed the frog I was holding onto so hard, I thought he was going to change shape permanently, his fat body becoming pinched in the middle as though he was wearing a corset. Chris held onto the two others, and the smallest one almost wiggled away from him several times.

"Here, put them in here," Matt said. He was holding out his lunch box, which had tumbled beside him on the ground.

These were pretty big frogs, not like the kind you find down by the lake. I couldn't fit all three in the lunch box. While Chris pushed the two he was holding onto in the box, I could tell the fat frog I was holding must be Joe. Even as a frog his eyebrows were crunched down on his eyes, looking real bully-like.

The smallest frog must be Sid, especially since it was dirtier than the rest. That was when I heard a low grumbly voice, "Hey, stop that!" I could recognize that voice anywhere. I turned around expecting to see Tom. Perhaps he wasn't a frog after all, but where was he? "Hey you scum, Let me go!"

"Chris, Matt, did you hear that?" I asked. "That frog's talking!"

"Of course I'm talking, you nerd. Let me go!" It was Tom, all right, wiggling with fury, trying to get out of Chris's hands. "Stop it! What do you mean, frog?"

"Wow, what a jerk. He doesn't even know he's a frog," Matt said. "Look at yourself, Tom. You're a frog. You're green and slimy and have ugly warts all over you," remarked Chris.

Now, I didn't like Tom, but I was kind of feeling sorry for him at this point. I mean, here he was a frog and all. And a real ugly frog at that. I don't think I would have rubbed it in about his warts, however. I handed the "Joe" frog to Matt, and helped Chris (who was having a time trying to handle two frogs), squish Tom and Sid into the lunch box. I snapped the lid tight. You could hear Tom and Sid in there, pushing each other around and arguing about who was the better looking frog. I thought that was kind of ridiculous, what with all that was happening.

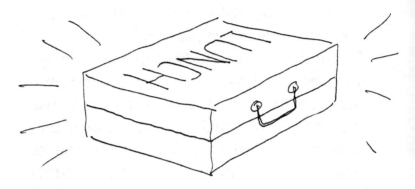

I couldn't fit the big old Joe frog in the lunchbox. It was just too big and fat. But he wasn't too bad looking for a frog. In fact, he was much better looking as a frog than he was as a kid. I was hanging on to him as tight as I could, but he was putting up quite a struggle.

"Chris, here. You better hang on to Joe. I gotta help Matt back up in his wheelchair," I said as I handed the big frog over to Chris.

The Joe frog hadn't said a thing. He was just fighting as hard as he could to get free. I went over to help Matt back into his chair.

"Thanks," Matt snapped at me as I tried to help him, "but I could of done this myself." He sounded put out with me just because I was trying to give him a hand. I don't know why someone would be mad when you are helping them.

It must be different when you are in a wheelchair. I mean, it must feel like you can't do anything yourself. Or that you have to prove you CAN do everything yourself. I don't know. I had to think about how it must be like in a wheelchair. I think that Matt really didn't want my help, or want me to think that he needed my help. But I still figured I'd better help him, since the chair was heavy and all. It's kind of a situation where you're darned if you do and you're darned if you don't. So, I tried to help him a little without making a big deal out of it.

"So, Matt, what do you think we should do with Joe?" I asked, trying to cover up how clumsy I felt and to get Matt's mind off of me helping him.

"How about usin' my lunch bag?" Chris volunteered. He handed the frog back to me while he took out the wrinkled-up bag out of his backpack. Chris held it out in triumph.

"Open it up so I can stick this frog in," I said.

Chris opened the bag and tried to straighten it out a little. I could see that something was still in the bag. "Yuck, there's a squished banana in there," I complained.

"What do you want me to do with it?" Chris asked, as he took it out and held it up with his thumb and forefinger.

"You're gross," I said, and shoved the "Joe" frog into the bag.

"Okay," said Matt, "we've got the frogs under control. But what are we going to do with them. We can't keep them like this, can we?"

But we didn't get to hang around there long enough to figure out what we were going to do. My sister Lora ran up to me, yelling, "Hurry, hurry! The bus is here."

I was going to have to run to catch the bus, plus Matt's mom was there to pick him up. So we quickly decided to meet after dinner at my house. Matt took his lunchbox with him and Chris took the bag with the "Joe" frog in it.

When I got onto the bus, I really had to roll my head around. My Tourettes was going crazy. I went through all sorts of tics while I was sitting there. And then an awful thought struck me: Chris still had the marble. What if he gets another big tic like that? What would happen? Who would he be pointing at?

I had to bury my head in my hands. I felt a Tourette attack coming on. I covered my ears to help drown out the sounds of the bus — 45 kids laughing and talking. I took deep breaths and waited for our bus stop.

Chapter 7

The Escape

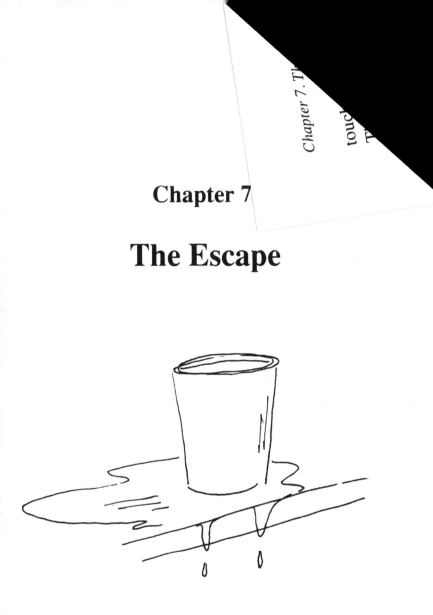

Lora put her hand on my shoulder. "Are you okay?" she asked? "You don't look so good. Are you having an attack?"

"Don't touch me," I snapped at her, "don't

me, don't touch me, don't touch me!"
This wasn't good at all. If we didn't get off the bus soon I might go into an all out rage attack from my Tourettes. I took a deep breath and tried to control myself. I tried to think good, calming thoughts as I prayed for that bus stop to get here soon.

The moment Lora and I were in the house, I ran into the kitchen to get a drink of Kool-aid. That was my mistake. I should have gone straight upstairs in order to rest. I knew it, but I tried to get my drink anyway. I knew I was asking for trouble.

"Oh shoot," I shouted as I spilled the Kool-aid over the edge of the cup. When you're having a Tourette attack any small thing can set you off. I started screaming. I could no longer talk. My mother ran in to see what was wrong.

"What happened?" she asked. "Calm down, Adam. Calm down. It's just a little Kool-aid. Try to pick up the dishcloth and clean it up."

She was trying to get me to help myself, but I kept screaming. I remember thinking, "Don't you know, a dishcloth won't work? It just pushes the Kool-aid around and makes a bigger mess?" but I couldn't say it. Of course, I wasn't thinking right. When you are in the middle of an attack, there is no reasoning. Sometimes I feel like I should slap myself. I started hitting myself on the side of my head, but it didn't knock out my Tourette attack at all. Now I just had a headache.

"Here is a paper towel. Is that what you want? Here honey, see if you can clean it up," my mom asked, trying to be as patient as possible.

I stopped screaming and defiantly grabbed the paper towel from her. I rubbed the spot hard and fast where the Kool-aid spill laid. I was successful in spreading the wet pool all over the counter, splashing some on the floor. I found small satisfaction in making a larger mess, but I didn't care.

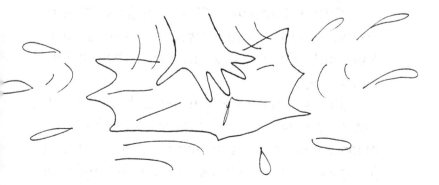

Well, my mom had about all she could stand at this point. She grabbed me and pulled me upstairs to my room. I tried hitting her. I don't know why. I didn't want to hit her, but I did anyway. It is like I can't stop myself when I'm like this. Then I was in my room. I slammed the door loudly behind me.

"I'm setting the timer for 20 minutes. We'll talk then," my mom shouted.

Okay. Now I've told you the real scoop around Tourette syndrome. It is miserable. That is why sometimes I try to hit my head — to knock it right out of me. I hope you understand that if it were up to me, I wouldn't have Tourette. But I'm stuck with it. It is a neurological disorder. I'm not going to die from it or anything. But I don't do these things on purpose. It's real hard for me to talk about it. This is what happens if I don't rest when I need to. But now I was grounded. My mom calls it "time-out".

Sometimes when I am in time-out, I sit up in my room and look out the window. I just look out like I am in a plane or something and I'm looking down at everyone. I don't say anything, so they don't know I'm looking. It's kind of like a time-out heaven, real quiet and peaceful. That's what I was doing when I saw Chris and Matt coming up the street. Matt had his lunch box in his lap and Chris was carrying his paper sack lunch-bag.

As they got closer I could see the bottom of Chris's lunchbag was very dark. It sort of looked like it was wet and soggy. Suddenly, a green frog leg popped out of the bottom of the bag.

"Chris!" I yelled. "Chris, the frog is getting out!" He looked up but he must not of heard what I said clearly because now there were two legs sticking out and he wasn't doing anything about it. "Chris! THE FROG IS GETTING OUT OF YOUR BAG!"

Matt heard me and looked over to the paper sack. "Chris," he yelled, "the bag!"

Chris grabbed at the bottom of the bag. But it was too late. The "Joe" frog had already leaped out and was hopping away. Chris scurried after the frog and Matt wheeled after the frog. Matt and Chris collided. Matt knocked into Chris, Chris fell over Matt. The two boys tumbled over the hedge our neighbor, Mr. Sowa, worked and labored over all summer. (It was a good thing Mr. Sowa wasn't around to witness this!)

All I could see now was four feet sticking out over the top of a giant hole in Mr. Sowa's poor old hedge. I could tell which one was Chris's feet because his big white shoes, the ones that had a little place on the tongue where you could pump them up with air to make them fit just right, were sticking straight out and kicking a lot. Matt's shoes were dangling under Chris's. It was the funniest thing. You had to laugh. But where were the frogs? I could see the lunch box sticking out of the hedge, but I couldn't make it out — was it opened?

I anxiously waited for the next few seconds to go by. I was helpless. I looked out of the window, stuck in my room, unable to do anything. I heard my mom yell up to me, "Adam! Be quiet up there. I want you to rest!"

"Hurry," I thought, "hurry and get up." Finally, Chris and Matt gathered themselves together. I held my breath. Chris helped Matt back into his chair. They started looking around the ground. "In the hedge!" I whispered, but they couldn't hear me.

"Here it is," said Matt. I could barely hear because they were so far away. He dug the lunch box out of the hedge. What I dreaded had happened. The lunch box was opened.

Chapter 8.

Dancing Fools

Matt and Chris looked up at my window. They knew I saw the whole thing. They looked so small down there. You could see the disappointment in their faces. They held the empty lunch box up so that I could see. From my window I had a view of the whole neighborhood. My eyes scanned everywhere — but there were no frogs to be seen. Tom, Joe, and Sid were gone!

I heard the buzzer go off downstairs. Finally, my 20 minutes of time-out were over. I ran down the stairs and headed toward the door.

"Wait a minute young man," my mom said. "Where do you think you're going?"

"The guys are outside, Mom. Can I play with them?" I asked, trying to sound as calm as possible. I knew that if I didn't sound calm, mom would make me stay in my room longer. "I feel fine now," and then I added for good measure, "Do you need me for anything?"

"Did you do your homework?"

"We didn't have any today. It's just the first day of school Mom." And then I thought of the perfect out. "But I brought home a ton of papers for you to fill out for school. They're in my backpack. You need to have them all done by tomorrow." I knew that would get her mind off of me. I reached in my backpack and handed her a pile of at least 50 papers. "You're supposed to read them all and sign them."

Well, that got her good. She sat down at the table and started looking through the pile.

Chapter 8. Dancing Fools

She was beginning to forget that I was in trouble. And then Lora came up behind her and said, "Yeah mom. I have a pile for you to read and sign too!"

My Mom put her hands up to her temples. She was getting a headache. It's pretty easy to give your mom a headache. Kids do it all the time. Mom looked at us, then at our piles of papers, and said, "Get out of here and go play, the both of you!" I was right. I figured she wouldn't want us around after that.

Once we were outside, Lora went to play with her friend across the street. I walked over to Chris and Matt. "I'm sorry," Matt pleaded. "They just got away."

"I'm sorry too," said Chris. In his hand was the old soggy paper bag. It really stunk.

"That bag is gross. It smells like an old rotten banana and a putrid frog," I complained. "Joe probably pee'd in it. Yuck. Throw it away."

"Eewe, he probably pooped in it too!" Matt said.

"Yeah, and he probably picked his frog nose with his slimey fingers and ate the boogers!" Chris exclaimed. Now they were getting too carried away with this, but it was kind of fun. "And then he pooped the boogers out!"

I was laughing so hard I could hardly breathe. "You guys are awful," I managed to get out between laughs. But, now what were we going to do? We really needed a plan. Chris was the first to stop joking and bring us down to reality.

"Okay, now what? What if Tom and Joe and Sid go tell the police? The police will come and get me. I'm cooked!" Chris was really getting excited. "I'm history! I'm going to be in prison for the rest of my life!"

I was worried about how anxious Chris was getting. He started shaking all over. "Where is the marble?" I thought, but it was too late. Chris was trembling and ticking. His body jerked forward and his hand reached out, pointing his finger before I could even take a breath. "CRACK!" A lightening bolt flew out of his glowing finger and lit toward Matt. I only had time to cover my eyes with my hands. I don't know what happened next. Everything seemed so loud for the next few seconds. I was afraid to open my eyes.

"Oh gee!" It was Chris speaking.

I opened my eyes and there was Matt, laid out on the ground. I breathed a sigh of relief. He wasn't a frog. "Thank goodness that he isn't a frog."

"But I knocked him on the ground. Maybe he's dead." Chris started crying. "I killed him."

Then Matt opened his eyes. He lifted himself up and looked at us. "What happened?" he asked. "Why am I down here?"

"Chris zapped you," I said.

"Well, am I a frog? Am I green?" Matt asked.

"Not yet," I said. "But I had better get that marble away from you, Chris, before you really do some damage." There was no telling what Chris might do or zap next. I put out my hand toward Chris. "Give it here."

"Sure! I don't want it." Chris was drying his eyes now. He was considerably shaken up. "I didn't mean it."

With the marble back in my own pocket, I bent over to pick up the wheelchair. Matt got up, walked over to the wheelchair and sat down in it.

THAT'S RIGHT. MATT WALKED!

Well, you can bet Chris and I were flabbergasted. Matt had walked over to his wheelchair just as casually as can be and sat down. He acted as just if it was as natural as 1, 2, 3.

"Matt! YOU WALKED!" I yelled at him as though he couldn't hear. "You walked! You walked!"

"What are you talking about?" he asked.

By now Chris and I had started dancing a little jig together. "You walked, you walked!" we were yelling. We were so excited, we couldn't stop. We jumped up and down and around in circles.

Matt looked at us as though we were crazy. Then he looked down at his legs. He moved his toes. He wiggled his feet. He kicked up his right foot into the air. He stood up and sat back down. He did this about five times. Then he stood up again and took two steps. Then he started walking. He started running. He started dancing with us!

"I can walk!" Mat shouted. "I can dance!"

We got so dizzy dancing around in circles that we fell onto the grass, laughing and being goofy. I guess we had forgotten all about the frogs by now. We had completely stopped thinking about how Chris might get arrested. We were just real happy.

What we hadn't noticed was that there were three pairs of suspicious little eyes staring at us from Mr. Sowa's hedge. Three pairs of eyes right under the big hole Matt and Chris made earlier. Two pairs just glaring and the third with little frowny eyebrows looking real mean and bully-like.

And, we didn't notice that the magic crystal marble had rolled out of my pocket as we hit the grass. In fact, it had rolled dangerously close to Mr. Sowa's hedge. Right where the big hole was.

Chapter 9.

Ghosts and Killers

We heard the laughing before we knew what happened. It came from behind the hedge.

"What is that?" I asked. It sounded like Joe's disgusting sneer mixed in the laughter. I felt my pocket — THE MARBLE WAS GONE! "My marble!"

Beyond the hedge we could see three frogs quickly leaping away and then they disappeared.

We all searched frantically for the marble. Behind every bush, every tree, every flower. Even under the weeds. But no marble. The frogs had taken it.

"Even as frogs they're jerks!" I shouted. "We have to find them."

"There's no telling what they might do with the magic of the marble," Matt said. "They might kill us all!"

The thought was certainly unsettling. We started toward the last spot we saw the frogs. "They headed this way," Chris said as he pointed down the lane. We looked at each other. All three of us whispered at the same time, "They're going to Dead Man's Lake!"

Now, you got to know that I really didn't believe the stories about the lake. I mean, after all, a 10 year old boy is too grown up to believe in ghosts. I knew there couldn't be ghosts at that lake, honest. And all those stories about killers hiding in the trees after dark - I think some really sick people made them up. It isn't possible, I was sure of it.

But it was the muddiest lake I had ever seen. It also had so many bugs around it that the people in our town talked about filling in the entire lake with dirt. The only reason they hadn't is because the environmentalists wouldn't let them. Something about a bird that stopped there during its nesting season. It was all quite complicated, but the muddy, buggy lake was still there. And that's where the frogs had gone.

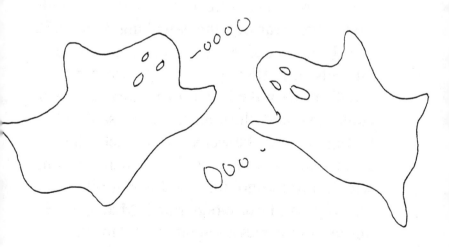

Even though I didn't believe the ghost and killer stories, I couldn't help feeling uneasy as we got closer to the edge of the lake. It was getting close to dark now and the shadows of the trees created a real eerie look to the entire area. The old trees appeared as though their leaves were dripping in the water, and the shadows, the leaves, and the surface of the water all blended together. Small gnats and probably mosquitoes were buzzing all around us. Boy, this was really a frog's paradise. I knew Joe, Tom, and Sid were lurking here somewhere.

"This ground sure is sticky," Matt said. You could hear our shoes making a "squish, squish" noise each time we picked up our feet. "It feels so neat!"

"You're weird," Chris remarked, but I could imagine how it must feel pretty good to be walking in mud after sitting in a wheelchair. In fact, when I was little I used to love to wiggle my toes in this mud and catch frogs with my dad. I was wondering if Matt had ever got to do this with his dad.

"How long have you been in a wheelchair?" I asked. "I mean, you know, have you ever been able to walk?"

"My legs just were never strong enough," Matt replied. "I have cerebral palsy. I was born with it. It's like a birth defect."

"Well, your legs look great now!" Chris said proudly. "My tics really paid off, didn't they."

Now, I haven't been telling you how much Chris and I tic. We tic all the time. Of course, it was only Chris's big giant shake that seemed to be magic when he had the marble. And I was beginning to think it was a good thing, cause if everytime he shook he did magic, there's no telling what could of happened.

"There's a frog!" Matt yelled. But it wasn't one of our frogs. It was the brown puny kind that I used to catch with my dad.

We kept looking. It was getting kind of late. The sun was down now and the light was fading. I thought of the killers and ghosts that probably hide in the dark.

A couple of hours had gone by since we started looking. I guess it was around 7:30 or so. In just a short while it would be dark. Our parents would start looking for us if we didn't show up soon. But we couldn't go back. Not without the frogs.

That was when we heard it. A low hum

coming through the trees. As we circled the lake, the sound became louder. I tried to make out what it was. Voices talking? Was it singing? It was so low that it was impossible to tell. We had to get closer.

We came to a row of trees and we could tell that whatever was making the noise must be just on the other side in the clearing on the edge of the lake. My knees trembled as we snuck up to peer over the low bushes by the trees. We tried not to make too loud of squishing noises as we crept. I felt short of breath. I hoped that we wouldn't be seen by whatever was making this low murmuring sound. You could hear it better now, and it seemed to be some kind of a song. Some kind of miserable, witch-chant. We reached out to move the branches of the nearest bush ever so slightly and quietly to see through.

Chapter 10.

The Zombies

The leaves parted as we pushed the branches open. I wasn't sure if I wanted to look. What if it were the killers or some awful kind of ghost. I hardly dared to breathe, that someone would hear.

There was light from a fire in the clearing. It sparkled and spit and lit the whole area with an eerie glow. It was the kind of perfect fire that you could sit by and tell gruesome ghost stories. The type of stories that sent shivers up your spine and kept you sleepless all night. The light of the fire revealed grotesque figures hopping and reeling around it in a circle. I could see quite well in the light and made out the ugliest group of animals I ever saw: three squirrels, two junkyard dogs, an alley cat, and an old haggard looking coyote. But these weren't ordinary looking animals. They were large, about the size of a man, and walked on their hind legs. Their eyes were glazed as if they were hypnotized, and their lips were drawn back to expose oversized teeth and fangs. They were chanting a song over and over, and I listened carefully to the words:

It's people we hate,
and we want to kill,
As many as possible
With our magic will
We'll bite off their heads,
To make our swill.
And eat their gizzards,

76

Till we have our fill
We'll rule the world
Make lots of noise
Hunt the girls
and find the boys
Kidnap them all
And take their toys
Cause it's people we
hate and want to kill
We will, we will
We will, we will!

I shuddered as the verse unfolded before me. It was the most frightful thing I had ever heard. My skin crawled as I wondered how this could be happening. Then, behind the circle of ghastly animals, I could see the answer to my question. There were Joe, Tom, and Sid, laying lazily by the dancing troupe, their green faces glowing in the flickering light.

"Chris, Matt, there they are!" I whispered.

"They must have used the magic to turn those animals into zombies!" Chris whispered back, his voice rasping with excitement, his body shaking and trembling.

"Yeah, they do look like zombies," Matt whispered. "What are we gonna do?"

A large gnat flew by Joe. We could tell it was Joe because of his crunched eyebrows. As the gnat neared him, his long frog tongue rolled out of his huge mouth and, SNAP, the gnat was gone.

"Did you see that?" Chris asked.

"Yeah," Matt answered. "That's gross. Can you imagine eating a fly?"

"No, not that, the marble," I said. I saw it. I was sure of it. When Joe's mouth opened you could see the magic crystal marble stuck right there in that huge mouth, right under his tongue. We saw it for just a fraction of a moment, but you couldn't miss it. His mouth opened again. You could see the marble glistening in the light as he snatched a moth in midflight.

"Wow. We gotta get the marble! Let's go over there." Matt said, and he pointed to a clump of bushes behind Joe. "Maybe we can grab him from over there."

As we carefully crawled over to our new location, my eyes were transfixed on the zombies and I caught a closer look. In fact, I couldn't look away. It was as if my eyes were frozen and I had to memorize every gruesome detail. Their glazed eyes stared blankly. I could see the dark of their pupils, which reflected the light of the fire like a mirror. They danced and sang as though they were under a powerful spell. My eyes were so stuck on those zombies, I almost tripped as we made our way to the bushes.

They were terribly horrifying, and looking at them gave me the shakes all over. These zombies were not the cute little animals you see in fairy stories or on T.V. They appeared to be mutants of some sort. I was hypnotized by the sheer horror of it.

To make matters worse, a lot worse, we suddenly heard a loud and slimey sounding "BEELLCCHH!"

"What was that?" Matt asked. We stopped

in our tracks. It was a huge burp, no, a long and drawn out BELCH. It was definitely the kind of belch that would win a belching contest. It put the ordinary, wrenching kind of belch, the kind you let go with after eating a big turkey dinner and your mother steps out of the room, to shame. It came from Joe, the belching king.

We had not quite reached the area behind Joe. At the sound of the disgusting belch, we quickly huddled into the nearest bush. We could see the animals clearly from this spot, and THEY WERE GROWING! I gasped as the thought hit me — Joe was making the zombies grow by burping!

We finally made it over to the bush behind the frogs. The three of them were grouped together, Joe in the middle, Sid on one side and Tom on the other. It was clear that Joe was the king-pin, lying there eating those disgusting flies.

Joe was only about three feet away from us, just about one good leap. With a good enough push I could probably grab him. Just as I was thinking of this, the frogs started talking.

"Boy this is gonna be great," Sid said. He was dirtier than ever, mud sticking to his green, slick skin. "We're gonna rule the world!"

"Yeah," said Tom. He began to lay down their plan. "Joe can put everyone under his spell. We can make everyone do whatever we want. We won't have to go to school or any-thing."

"And if they don't obey us, SNAP!" Sid said as he tried to snap his slimey frog fingers. "We'll have them taken care of."

Joe didn't say anything, probably because of the marble in his mouth. He just let out a deep sinister chuckle.

Chris, Matt, and I looked at each other

frantically. Joe let out another belch: "BEELLCCHH!" The animal zombies were getting to be about 8 or 9 feet tall, their grotesque features getting larger and larger.

We had to stop Joe, and we had to stop him now!

Chapter 11.

Powerful and Dangerous Magic

It was amazing the magic of that marble. In just one day the best things and the worst things had happened to us. The power of the marble was great and dangerous. It wasn't ordinary magic. Not the kind you read about in story books. This was real, awful, powerful, not always good magic. In story books the magic is always good or always evil. But this crystal marble magic knew no bounds.

I felt like I was trapped in a horror movie or a nightmare. In either case, I could hardly stand it. I can't even stand to watch a scary movie, or even one that has someone dying in it. I think it's my Tourette syndrome. I get real upset and have to turn off the T.V. I would never go to a movie like this. But it wasn't a movie, this was real.

I took a step back and rolled my head three or four times. I stretched and clenched my finger another ten times at least. I felt like I might wet my pants any moment, but I was as ready as I would ever be. I leaned forward to brace myself for running. Matt and Chris looked at me. We didn't speak, but all of us knew what had to be done, and I was going to do it.

The only thing I heard was that Joe frog belching real loud again. I sprang forward and took the longest leap I could. My feet landed in the mud, my body fell forward, and my hands wrapped around Joe. Mud was everywhere. The marble flew right out of his mouth and disappeared into the soggy blackness of the mud. I couldn't waste any time. My hands groped in that black slime for the marble. I looked up to see the zombies growing, but I hadn't time to think about it.

I FOUND THE MARBLE!

"Hurry Adam!" I heard Chris and Matt

yell at me. I clutched the marble and it grew hot in my hand. As I made my way back to the bushes I could see the frogs jumping all around me. I could just make out the towering zombie shapes coming toward me.

"Oh geez! They're gonna kill us!" Chris screamed. "Hurry Adam!"

I reached the bushes and we all ran together, away from this dark and evil place. We knew the zombies were chasing us. We knew they would overtake us soon. We had to think fast.

"I have a plan!" Matt shouted at us as we ran. "You have to get rid of the marble. You have to destroy it now!"

He was right. We couldn't let the zombies have it. We couldn't let anyone have this magic, a magic that could be so evil it would ruin the world. We ducked into the cover of a bush. In the darkness of the night we could barely see the zombies pass us, but we could hear them. Chris had found a large flat rock. Matt found a smaller one. I held the marble.

"Quick, Adam. Put the marble on the rock!" Chris whispered as he held the smaller one high, ready to bring it down with crushing force.

I held the marble in my hand and felt its heat. Its bright glow was casting a light about us. I could see the flat rock clearly, but I hesitated. I looked up in the direction of the rustling sounds, which were coming towards us. The branches of our bush shook and then parted. A huge zombie, one that resembled a 10 foot squirrel, was glaring at us. His sharp teeth glistened against the dark sky from the glow of the marble. One paw reached for us with claws extended.

I placed the marble on the rock. "Crush it now!" I yelled at Chris.

The zombie's claws swiped in the air by my head as I ducked. The rock came out hard. I saw a bright fiery flash of light brightened the entire area. It glowed and then grew dim. A few glittery sparkles of light floated in the air. And then, silence...

We hadn't thought about what would happen next. All was quiet except for a chirping of crickets. My ears rang. Crouched in the darkness, Chris, Matt, and I could barely see each other, the glow from the marble gone.

"Wow." I sighed. "What happened?"

"They're gone," Matt said.

"Yeah, they're all gone," Chris added. "I

feel like, I don't know." His body jerked forward. "My Tourette's driving me crazy."

"Let's go home," Matt said.

We got up and pushed our way out of the bush. Chris and I took a few steps, then looked at each other. "Where's Matt?" I asked. I looked back at the bush. "Come on Matt."

We waited, but he didn't come out. I pushed my way back into the thickness of the branches. "What's going on?" I asked.

Matt looked up at me. "I can't," he said. "I can't move my legs."

Chris had crept in behind me now and we both dropped to our knees. We stayed there for a long time, kneeling by Matt. We didn't say anything — we couldn't. We just stayed there while the darkness crept in around us.

I gazed at the slivers of crystal still laying on the rock where the marble had been crushed. They were tiny little pieces, rounded sort of, picking up the barest light from the stars. They reminded me of fairy dust. I gathered the three largest pieces and put them in my pocket.

We finally helped Matt up and between Chris and me, we managed to carry, drag, and pull Matt back to the edge of the woods. Once we got to the street, Chris ran ahead of us to get the wheelchair.

As we helped Matt into his wheelchair (he didn't protest this time), I remembered the pieces of crystal in my pocket. I reached in and pulled them out. "I picked these up," I said. "We can keep them to remember tonight."

"I don't think I'll ever forget," Chris remarked. He reached for his crystal piece anyway.

Matt put his crystal sliver in his pocket. He hadn't said anything since we left the bushes. Chris and Matt took off, heading towards their houses. "I'll see ya tomorrow," I yelled. Chris waved back, then they were gone in the darkness.

I went into my own house. Mom was pretty upset that I was back so late. I was dead tired, so I went upstairs to my room. I couldn't believe everything that happened that day. I was exhausted. I think I fell asleep before my head hit the pillow. I just remember thinking about what must have happened to Joe, Tom, and Sid. Where were they?

Chapter 12.

Feeling Great

The next morning I awoke feeling great. I can't describe it, except that it was just a feeling of waking up and having a bright sunny day greet you. I felt good.

Lora and I had to walk to the bus stop. I hadn't even tried to tell Lora or my mom and dad what happened the day before. I figured it was so far fetched that they wouldn't believe me.

Lora complained when we left. She wanted dad to drive us. I would have let him gladly, but he was still taking his shower. We had to walk.

As we got closer to the bus stop, Lora stopped. "Look Adam," she said. "Look, there's those mean guys. I don't want to go any further."

They were there, all right. Not as the slimey green frogs with slick, shiny skin that I saw last night. No, today they looked like regular kids, at least as regular as Joe, Tom, and Sid could ever look. It was as though last night never happened. I thought about turning around and running. Or climbing up the nearest tree where they couldn't reach me. The events of yesterday were so fresh in my mind that a chill ran up my back.

I put my hand in my pocket to feel the small piece of crystal — the only remnant of our adventure. Yes, it was there. In the deep corner of my pocket, amid the fuzz and threads and little chunks of sand that normally live there.

I didn't run. I didn't hide in the upper branches of the nearest tree. I don't know why, but there was a feeling in me that told me I had to face whatever was going to happen. I had to go on and walk all the way to the corner of the bus stop, no matter what. I had to go on.

There's really no way I can explain why the next thing happened. Lora and I walked right up to the bus stop. Joe, Tom, and Sid just looked at us and said "Hi." I don't know why. They didn't tease me or try to beat me up or anything. They just said "Hi", and went on talking to each other. Five minutes went by. The rest of the kids got there and the bus came, and Joe, Tom, and Sid just got on the bus. Joe didn't spit or burp or nothing. It was weird. No fuss, no fight.

I felt relieved, and I still felt great, but I also got this funny kind of feeling. The kind of feeling you get when you're reading a real good book and you get to the ending and it just leaves you hanging there. It doesn't give you a good ending or a sad ending, just no ending at all. As though you're supposed to guess what happens next.

When we got to school, I got off the bus and watched Lora head for her classroom. I watched as Joe, Tom, and Sid got off quietly and silently headed for their classes. I stood there with this calm feeling, kind of like everything was okay, but also kind of like I was removed from my body and just watching. It was real strange, like a dream. I was prepared for the worst, and now nothing bad was going to happen after all.

As I walked down the hall, Chris ran up to me. He was obviously excited about something. "I feel great!" he said. "I feel like shouting!"

"Why? What's goin' on?" I asked. "Don't you know? Don't you feel great?" Chris asked me back. "Don't you feel different?"

"Yeah, sorta," I replied. "Why?"

"Well, MY TICS ARE GONE!" Chris

answered. "I thought maybe yours were too. Look it. Nothin'. No shakes. No tics. I can do anything." He jumped up and down.

I guess I just hadn't noticed before. I hadn't had a tic all morning. I mean, I guess maybe they WERE gone. "You're right," I told him. I haven't had any tics at all." I thought back about how easy it was for me to get ready this morning. No tics. No frustrations. No rages. No crying as I picked out my clothes to wear. Everything was so easy this morning I hadn't even noticed. NO TOURETTE SYNDROME!

"I think it's our little chunk of the marble," Chris said. "I think it's just the right size, just a little bit of the right kind of magic."

We walked into the classroom. I did feel good. In fact, I was feeling better all the time. I just couldn't believe that my Tourettes could be gone. "What about Matt?" I asked Chris. "Can he walk?"

But we didn't need to ask Matt that question. The answer was obvious when Matt came into the classroom...

...in his wheelchair.

Chris went over to him. I stayed my ground. I couldn't tell him about our Tourette syndrome being gone. His face was so expressionless, I could only aim my eyes at my desk. The magic crystal sliver hadn't worked for him. He was worse off than just having Tourette. He needed more than just a tiny chunk of magic in order to walk again.

Chris and I sat outside on the bench at lunchtime. Matt tucked his chair under the end of the table. We barely talked to each other as we ate our lunches.

"I have an idea!" Chris blurted out with a mouthful of food. "Let's give our pieces of the marble to Matt. Maybe he needs all three to help him walk!"

"Don't even try," Matt said. He turned his chair from the table and rolled away, leaving an uneaten half of peanut butter and jelly sandwich on the table.

"Well, I thought it was a good idea," I said. Of course, if it worked, it would mean giving Matt our pieces of crystal. That would mean that Chris and I would have Tourette syndrome again. My hand went to the hard sliver of crystal in my pocket. I must be a terrible person, because I honestly felt happy right then and there that Matt didn't want our pieces. I didn't want to give up my magic. I felt ashamed that I wanted to be free from my Tourettes, but wanting that meant that Matt wouldn't walk.

I may be 10 years old and almost grown-up, but I was feeling like I was awful little, too little to make this decision. It wasn't fair. I didn't want to make the decision, so I was glad Matt made it for me.

All day Matt's decision kept haunting me. There he was, stuck in his wheelchair with his cerebral palsy. Unable to walk with his weak legs. Unable to ever run through the woods and catch the lake frogs with his dad. Unable to scramble after a snake or a lizard. I just couldn't figure it. Why had he refused to take the magic?

I know it was wonderful that I no longer had Tourette syndrome. I really did feel that I was freed from an evil curse. On one hand I should be overjoyed. Yet, something bothered me that I couldn't shake.

By the end of the first week of school I was a wreck. I was doing great in school and everything, but I was obsessed with thoughts of Matt being unable to walk. Why had he refused the magic? There he sat at the back of the classroom, quiet and withdrawn. I just couldn't stand it anymore. Could it be he didn't want to find out that, even with the three pieces of magic marble, he wouldn't be able to walk? Or that something else might happen? But, whatever I thought, I kept coming back to what I felt was the real reason, the scariest one for me — he wouldn't try because if it did work, and he kept the marble pieces, Chris and I would get our Tourettes back.

He refused because he was our friend.

That Friday afternoon in class, I watched Matt working on his assignment in the back row of the room. It was just a few minutes before the final bell. I looked at his shoes. I must have a thing about shoes. I mean, I can usually tell how fun a kid is right away by looking at his shoes. If they are scuffed up and dirty, well, the kid must be a lot of fun. If they are neat and shiny, then the kid must be boring and studious.

I mean, Matt's shoes were real neat. They were cool-looking shoes and all, but they would never get worn out. He would just outgrow them and then get a new pair. He would never get a new pair because he wasted and ruined the pair he had. I always figured it was kind of a sin for a kid to have a pair of shoes that looked new. Mine always looked well used, even on the first day I put them on. It's like you're not having fun or doing the right kind of kid things if your shoes look new. Your just not doing your job right unless you've used your shoes to scuff up dirt, jump in puddles, slide on grass, and climb trees with them.

But that was the fate of Matt's shoes. Just to sit there real clean-like. To never get a hole and to never get wornout. I couldn't stand it.

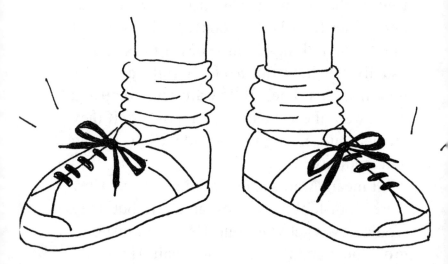

Chapter 13.

Old and Worn-out Shoes

Well, something just had to be done about those shoes. I took out a piece of paper from my notebook and, while Mrs. Keller was up there in the front of the class, writing on the chalkboard, I folded that piece of paper into a nice neat little envelope. I reached into my pocket, pulled my magic crystal sliver out, and slipped it into that envelope. My magical sliver that took my Tourette syndrome away. I closed the envelope tight and wrote CHRIS on it. Then I passed it quietly to the girl on my right.

And, just like that, it started. The fateful passing of the secret note. It always amazed me how a whole classroom of kids would know just what to do when a note was passed to them. My secret note slipped from one desk to the next, from one hand to the next. Without a sound, it was passed, without being opened and no questions asked. It stopped at Chris's desk.

Chris opened the small folded envelope and peered inside. He immediately put his hand into his pocket, pulled out his bit of magic, and added it to mine. He closed the envelope tight and wrote something on it. Looking at me and smiling, he passed the note to the kid behind him.

I held my breath as the note silently made its way to the back of the room. I finally took a breath when the note landed safely on Matt's desk. He looked up at it, and at that moment the bell rang.

Everyone shuffled out of the classroom. All that remained were Chris, Matt, me, and, of course, Mrs. Keller busily cleaning off the chalkboard.

Chris and I sat there in silence, waiting for Matt to move. He picked up the envelope and began to open it. I was on pins and needles as he stared at the contents. I rolled my head twice.

"Well," Chris said. "Come on Matt. Try it. Try to walk."

Matt reached into his pocket and pulled out the third sliver. He turned over the envelope and poured the other two onto his palm, so that now he was holding all three. They glistened and sparkled. I could of sworn I saw a glow as he closed his fist around the crystal pieces.

"Come on Matt, try to get up!" I said. "Try to walk. Please Matt."

"What are you children doing?" Mrs. Keller asked. You could tell she was concerned. "I thought you boys were friends of Matt's. Don't tease him. Don't..."

But she stopped in mid-sentence, and Chris and I stopped in mid-breath. Matt was getting up. He lifted himself right up and was standing all by himself. Mrs. Keller's mouth dropped open.

"Walk Matt!" both Chris and I shouted. "You can do it!"

Even Mrs. Keller was getting into the excitement of everything. "Yes, Matt. Try it," she said. "Come on."

Matt took a step. "It's amazing," Mrs. Keller was saying. Matt took another step. His fist was clenched tight around the magic slivers. HE COULD WALK. Well, that was one of the best days in my life. Sure, I got my Tourettes back. But how bad is that, really? I mean, it's not like I'm going to die from it or anything. Nobody seems to mind (except of course when I go into a rage), and I have lots of friends. I can run and swim. And, now, so can Matt.

That weekend we played around and climbed trees. All of Chris's shakes were back, and mine were too, but no one seemed to notice. Chris said that between us two, we were "shakin' fools."

"Wanna go to the lake?" Matt asked. "Maybe we can scrape up enough of the crystal pieces to fix you and Chris."

So, off we went to the lake. It took a couple of hours to find the spot where Chris had broken the marble. It's funny how different places can look in the daylight. The lake didn't seem scary or frightening now. Yet, I still got shivers running down my spine when we found the two rocks. It was strange, though, because there was no trace of the crystal. Not any dust or little bits of broken pieces.

"Where did the rest of the crystal pieces go to?" Matt asked. We didn't find out, though.

It was about a month later, when we were climbing up the big old tree in Mr. Sowa's yard that I noticed them again. Matt was climbing up ahead of me and I saw them real good. Matt's shoes. They were dirty and all torn up. Mud was caked on the side of them and one of the rubber soles were separating slightly. I guess you'd say that they was the most awesome shoes I ever saw.

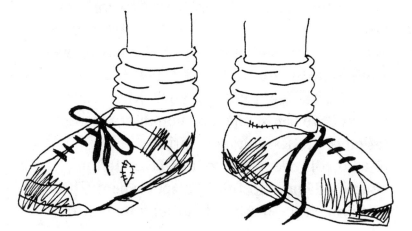

And at school... well, Joe, Tom, and Sid never picked on us again. We never really did figure out why. At first I thought it had something to do with the crystal, but since we had given all our crystals to Matt, I really don't know what caused the change. I'd see Joe every so often, walking down the hall at school, burping a little. He was pretty weird. I think he never got over being a frog. I think he was real happy that way. If you watched him very closely, and very carefully, you'd even see him rolling out his tongue and catching a fly. I swear.

As for Chris and me, well, we went through some pretty tough times, having strange tics from our Tourettes. I still had outbursts, but I practiced using time-outs whenever possible. It really seemed to help. Both of us worked real hard at controlling ourselves and teaching other people about Tourette syndrome. We were really growing up.

Then some pretty strange things started happening down by the lake. Evidently, a group of students went there for a field trip to collect some bugs. What they found were the biggest butterflies ever. These butterflies are about one foot across, and the most beautiful colors. All of the colors in the rainbow. Matt, Chris, and I went down to see them, and sure enough, there are some pretty strange things happening down there.

Last Saturday we saw a bright colored lizard in blue, green, and purple. I never saw anything like it before. Matt ran after it and caught it. We're going down there again tomorrow. We figure it's the crystals. Looks like we've got some adventures ahead of us.

We're going to find those magic crystals this time...